W9-AGZ-927

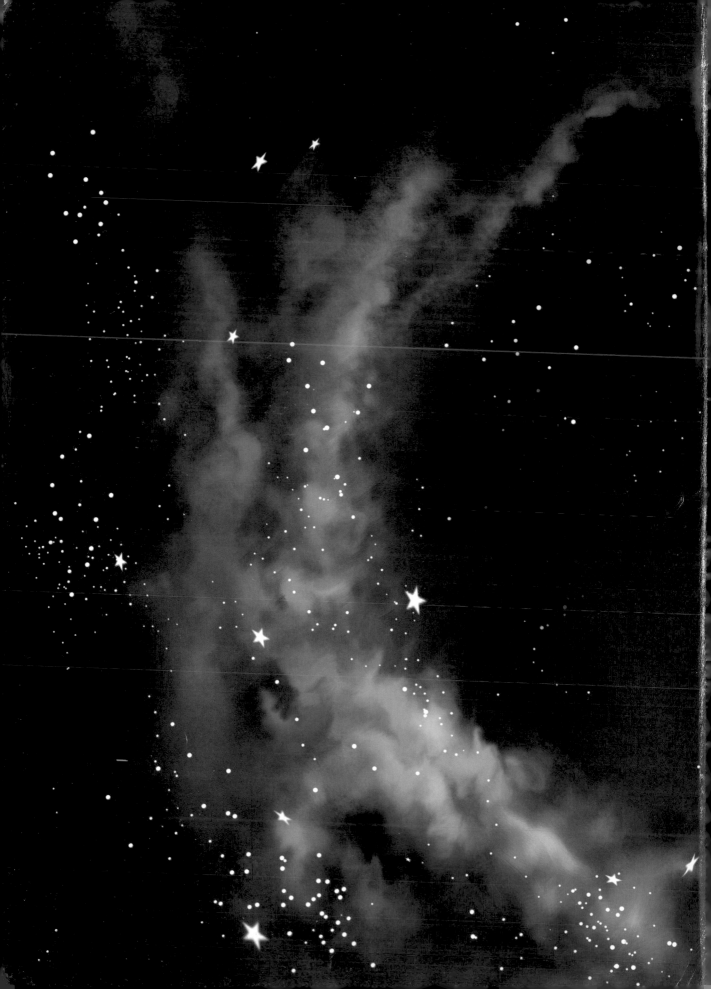

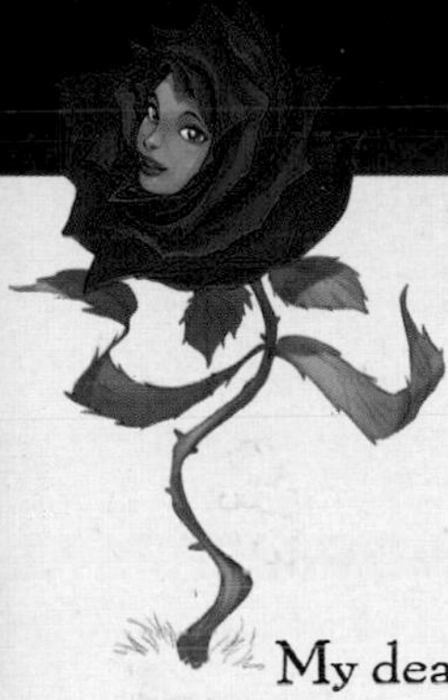

My dear Rose,

The planet of Ludokaa was full of surprises, including the most astonishing sunset I have ever seen!

Unfortunately, the sunset was so enchanting that the planet's inhabitants fought for the privilege of viewing it. I'm happy to say that they were able to set aside their differences and learn to enjoy the wonders of their planet together.

It is a rare privilege to share with others the feelings produced by such beauty. In fact, sharing a beautiful thing with others makes it even more beautiful.

If only the Snake could learn this lesson!

The Little Prince

First American edition published in 2014 by Graphic Universe™.

Le Petit Prince ™

based on the masterpiece by Antoine de Saint-Exupéry

© 2014 LPPM
An animated series based on the novel *Le Petit Prince* by Antoine de Saint-Exupéry
Developed for television by Matthieu Delaporte, Alexandre de la Patellière, and Bertrand Gatignol
Directed by Pierre-Alain Chartier

© 2014 ÉDITIONS GLÉNAT
Copyright © 2014 by Lerner Publishing Group, Inc., for the current edition

Graphic Universe™
A division of Lerner Publishing Group, Inc.
241 First Avenue North
Minneapolis, MN 55401 U.S.A.

Website address: www.lernerbooks.com

Library of Congress Cataloging-in-Publication Data

Bruneau, Clotilde.
    [Planète des Lacrimavoras. English]
    The Planet of Tear-eaters / story by Delphine Dubos ; design and illustrations by Elyum Studio ; adaptation by Clotilde Bruneau ; translation, Anne Collins Smith and Owen Smith. — 1st American ed.
        p.   cm. — (The little prince ; #13)
    ISBN 978—0—7613—8763—3 (lib. bdg. : alk. paper)
    ISBN 978—1—4677—2423—4 (eBook)
    1. Graphic novels. I. Dubos, Delphine. II Smith, Anne Collins. III. Smith, Owen. IV. Elyum Studio.
V. Petit Prince (Television program) VI. Title.
PZ7.7.B8Pm 2014
741.5'944—dc23   2013014075

Manufactured in the United States of America
1 — PC — 12/31/13

THE NEW ADVENTURES
BASED ON THE MASTERPIECE BY ANTOINE DE SAINT-EXUPÉRY

The Little Prince

THE PLANET OF TEAR-EATERS

Based on the animated series and an original story by Delphine Dubos

Design: Elyum Studio
Story: Clotilde Bruneau
Artistic Direction: Didier Poli
Art: Diane Fayolle
Backgrounds: Isa Python
Coloring: Moonsun
Editing: Christine Chatal
Editorial Consultant: Didier Convard

Translation: Anne and Owen Smith

Graphic Universe™ • Minneapolis

★ THE LITTLE PRINCE

The Little Prince has extraordinary gifts. His sense of wonder allows him to discover what no one else can see. The Little Prince can communicate with all the beings in the universe, even the animals and plants. His powers grow over the course of his adventures.

The Prince's uniform:
When he transforms into the uniform of a prince, he is more agile and quick. When faced with difficult situations, the Little Prince also uses a sword that lets him sketch and bring to life anything from his imagination.

His sketchbook:
When he is not in his Prince's clothing, the Little Prince carries a sketchbook. When he blows on the pages, they take wing and form objects that he'll find very useful. Like his sword, it's powered by stardust collected on his travels.

★ FOX

A grouch, a trickster, and, so he says, interested only in his next meal, Fox is in reality the Little Prince's best friend. As such, he is always there to give him help but also just as much to help him to grow and to learn about the world.

★ THE SNAKE

Even though the Little Prince still does not know exactly why, there can be no doubt that the Snake has set his mind to plunging the entire universe into darkness! And to accomplish his goal, this malicious being is ready to use any form of deception. However, the Snake never takes action himself. He prefers to bring out the wickedness in those beings he has chosen to bite, tempting them to put their own worlds in danger.

★ THE GLOOMIES

When people who have been ''bitten'' by the Snake have completely destroyed their own planets, they become Gloomies, slaves to their Snake master. The Gloomies act as a group and carry out the Snake's most vile orders so he can get the better of the Little Prince!

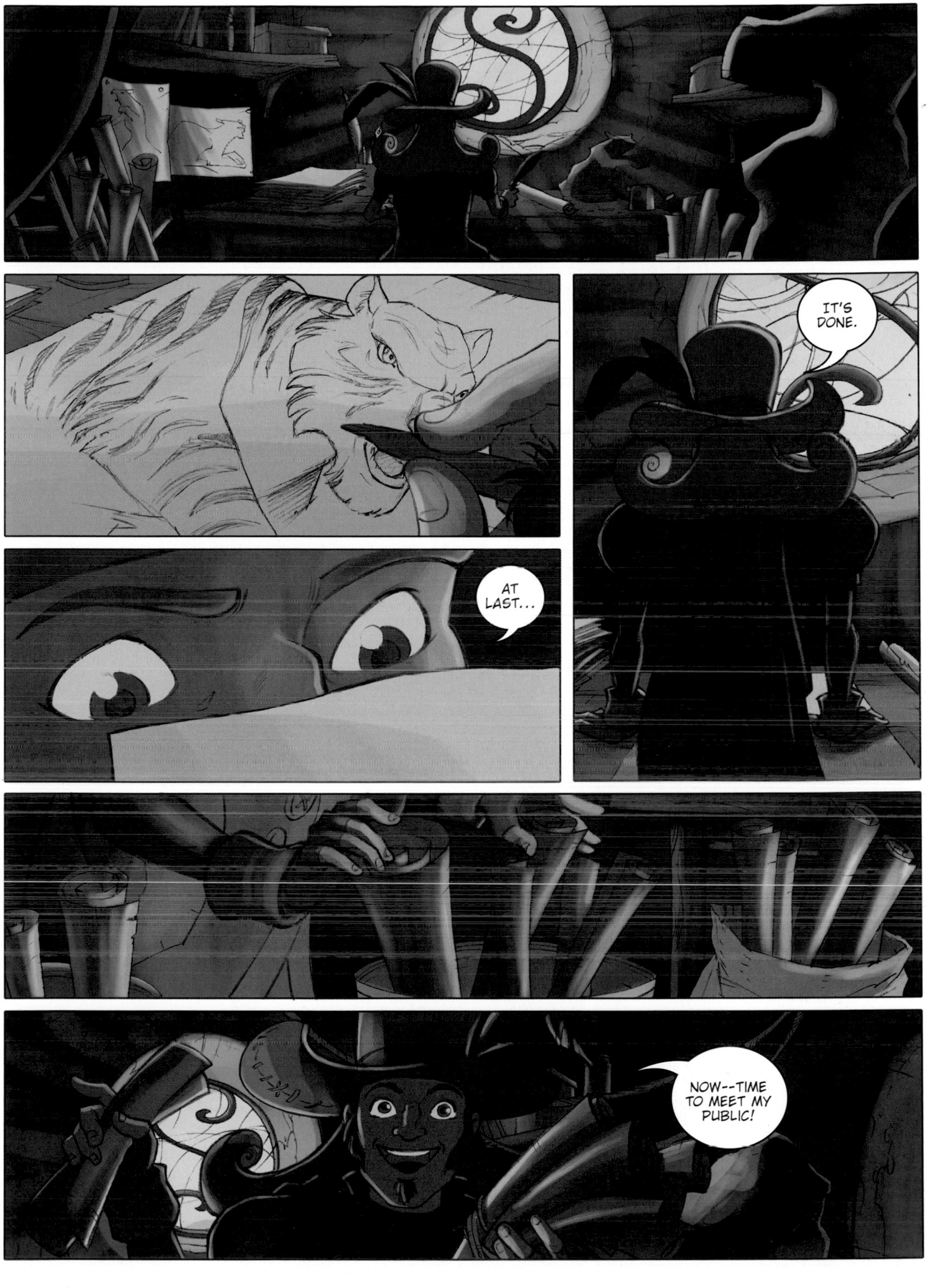
IT'S DONE.
AT LAST...
NOW--TIME TO MEET MY PUBLIC!

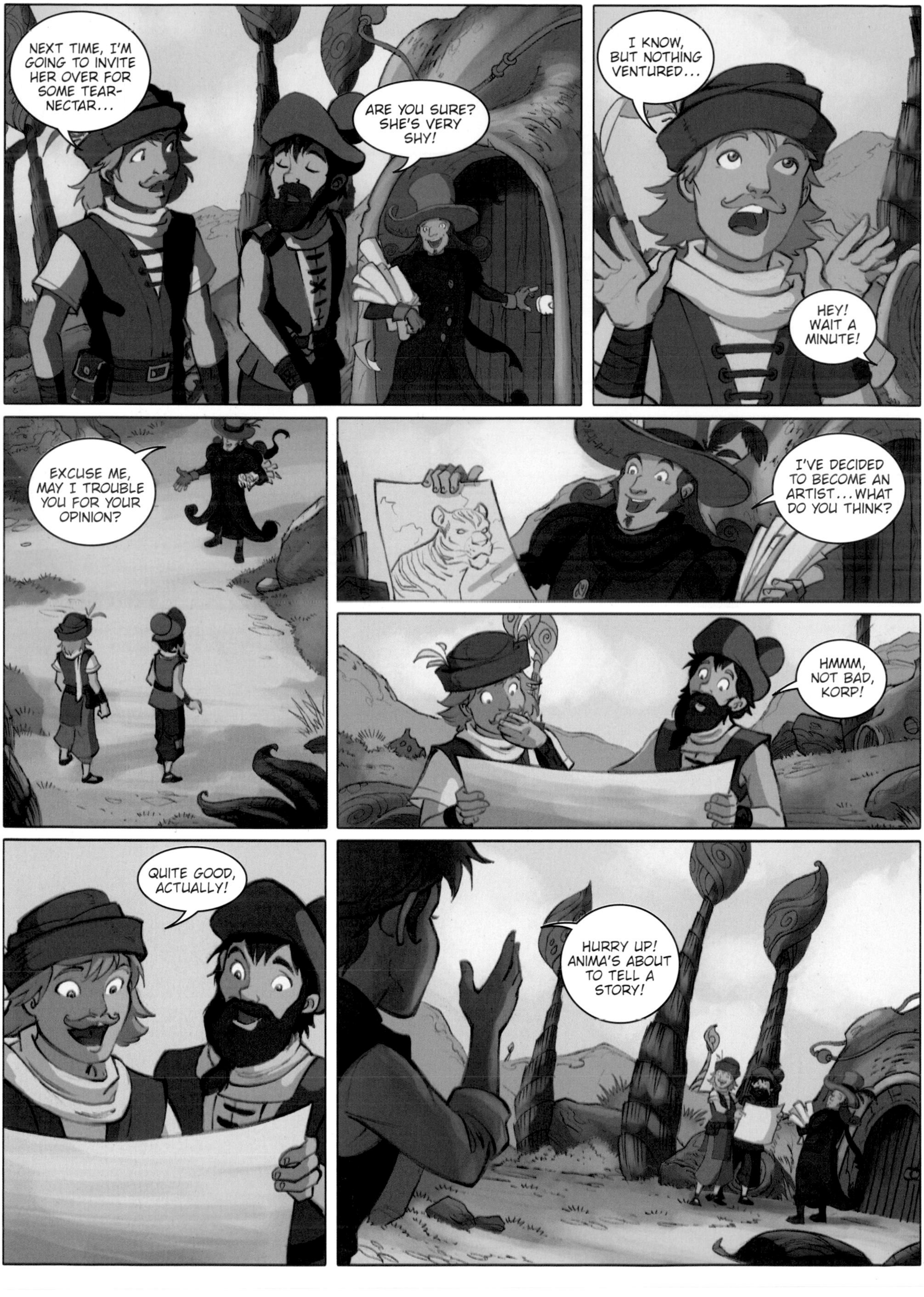
NEXT TIME, I'M GOING TO INVITE HER OVER FOR SOME TEAR-NECTAR...
ARE YOU SURE? SHE'S VERY SHY!
I KNOW, BUT NOTHING VENTURED...
HEY! WAIT A MINUTE!
EXCUSE ME, MAY I TROUBLE YOU FOR YOUR OPINION?
I'VE DECIDED TO BECOME AN ARTIST... WHAT DO YOU THINK?
HMMM, NOT BAD, KORP!
QUITE GOOD, ACTUALLY!
HURRY UP! ANIMA'S ABOUT TO TELL A STORY!

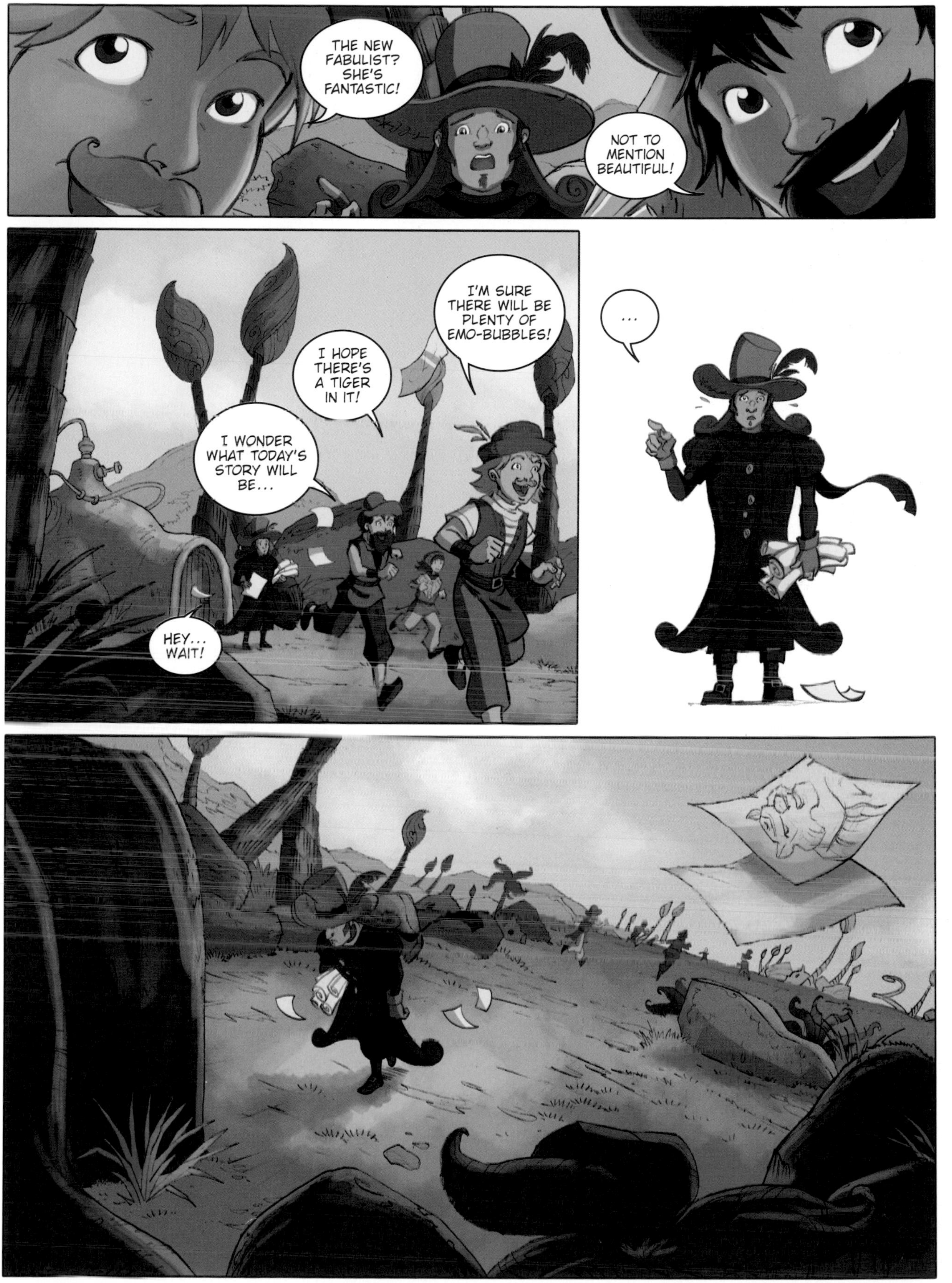
THE NEW FABULIST? SHE'S FANTASTIC!
NOT TO MENTION BEAUTIFUL!
I WONDER WHAT TODAY'S STORY WILL BE...
I HOPE THERE'S A TIGER IN IT!
I'M SURE THERE WILL BE PLENTY OF EMO-BUBBLES!
HEY... WAIT!
...

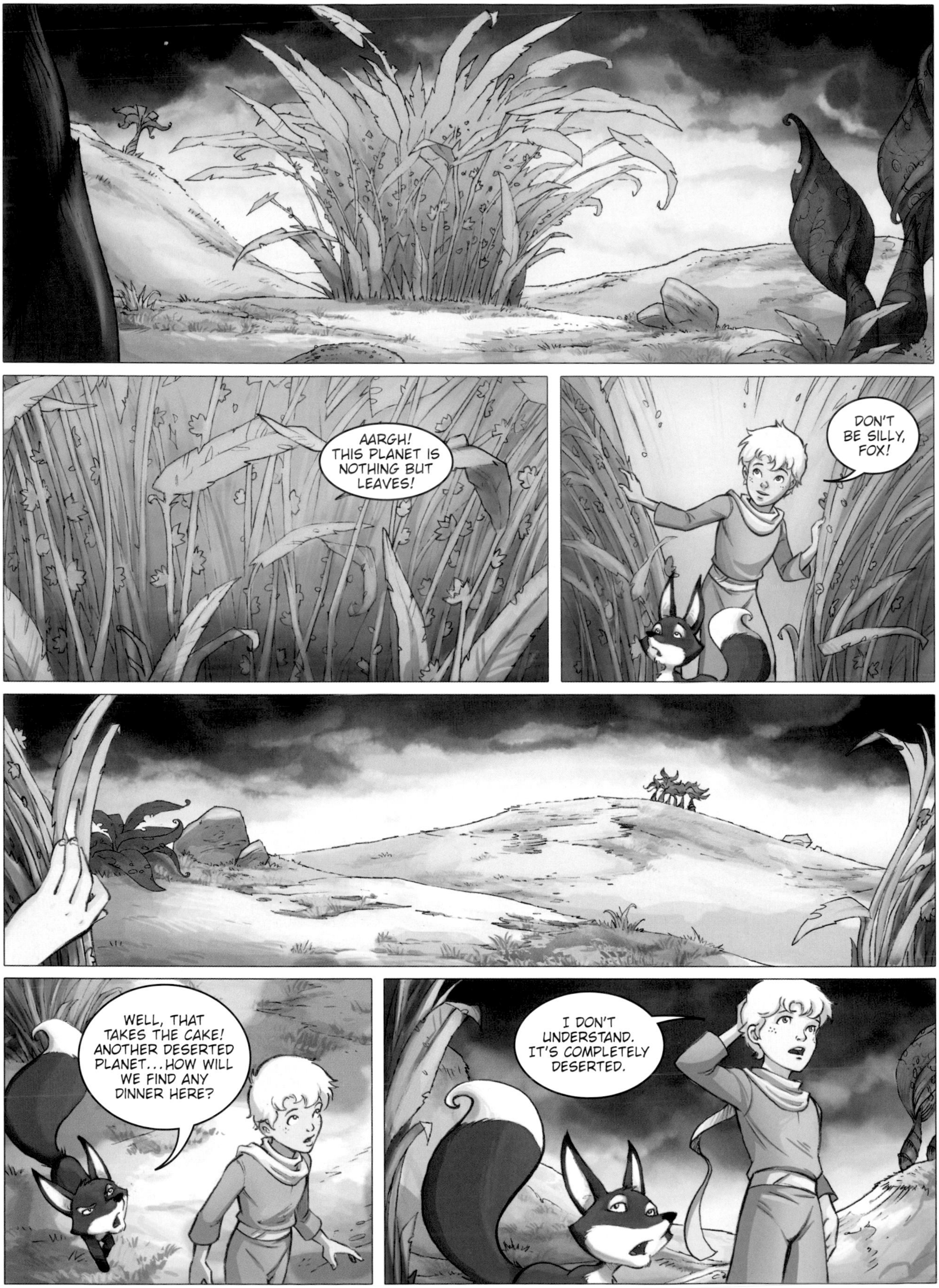
AARGH! THIS PLANET IS NOTHING BUT LEAVES!
DON'T BE SILLY, FOX!
WELL, THAT TAKES THE CAKE! ANOTHER DESERTED PLANET...HOW WILL WE FIND ANY DINNER HERE?
I DON'T UNDERSTAND. IT'S COMPLETELY DESERTED.

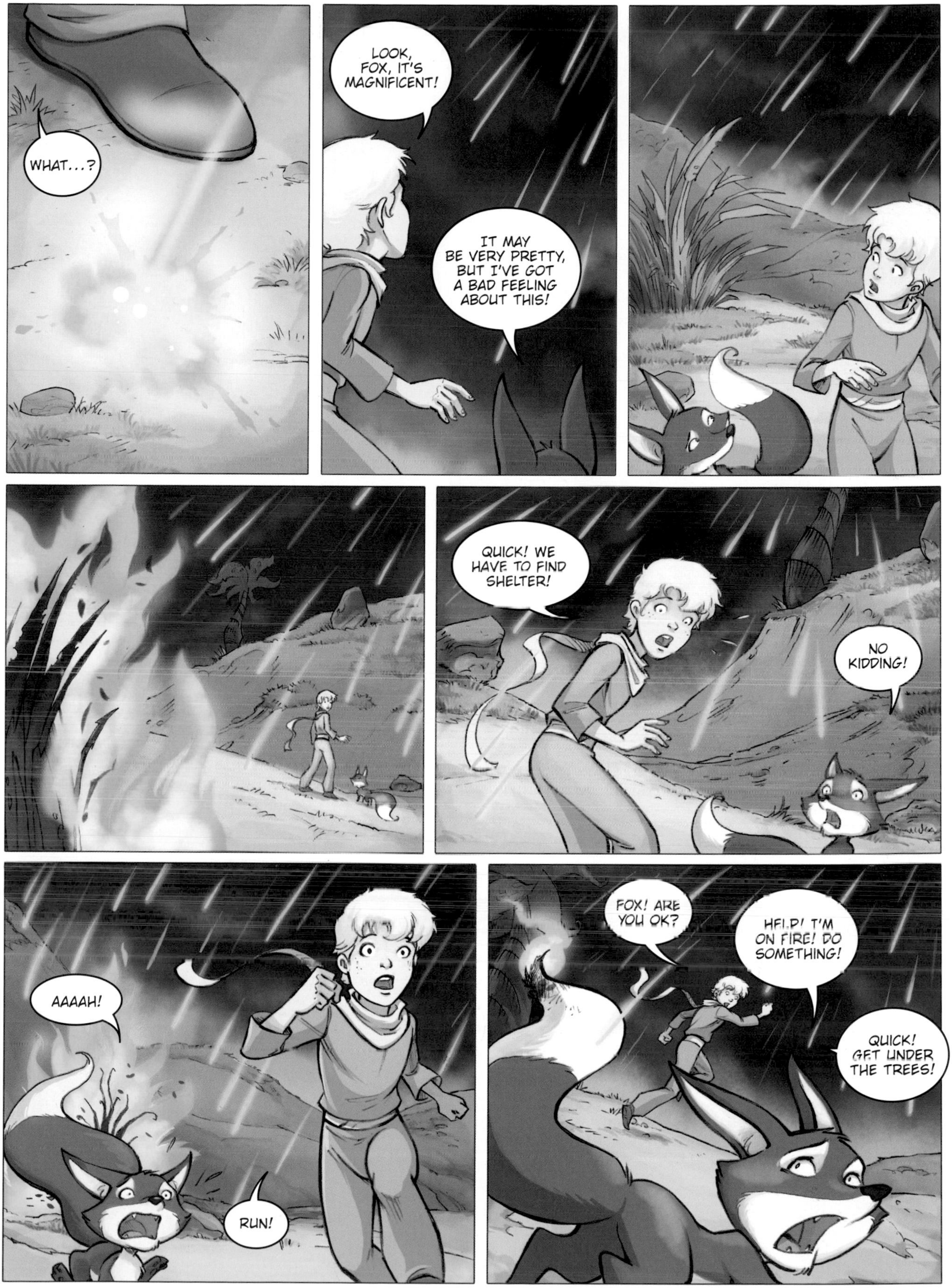
WHAT...?
LOOK, FOX, IT'S MAGNIFICENT!
IT MAY BE VERY PRETTY, BUT I'VE GOT A BAD FEELING ABOUT THIS!
QUICK! WE HAVE TO FIND SHELTER!
NO KIDDING!
AAAAH!
RUN!
FOX! ARE YOU OK?
HELP! I'M ON FIRE! DO SOMETHING!
QUICK! GET UNDER THE TREES!

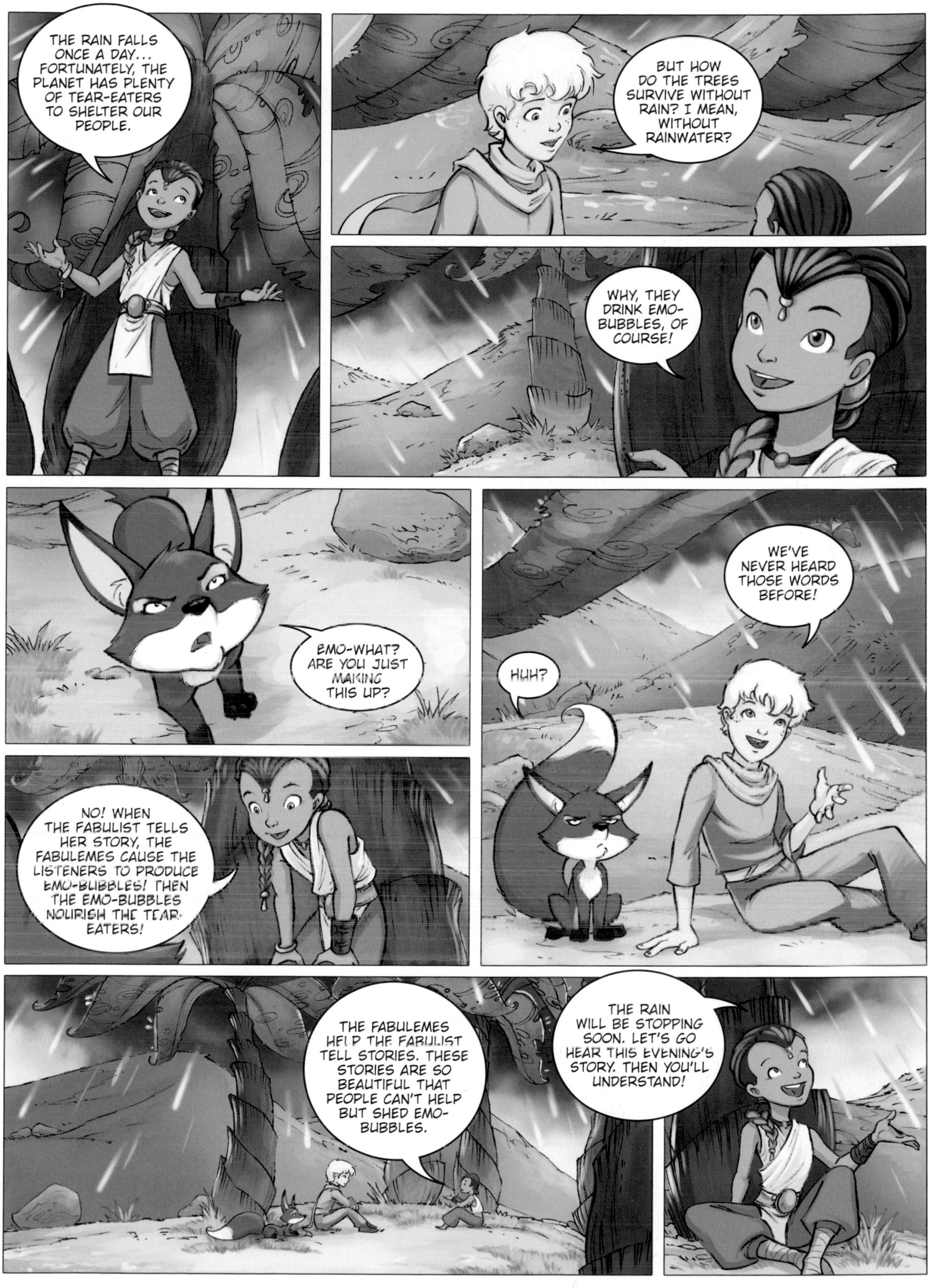
THE RAIN FALLS ONCE A DAY... FORTUNATELY, THE PLANET HAS PLENTY OF TEAR-EATERS TO SHELTER OUR PEOPLE.
BUT HOW DO THE TREES SURVIVE WITHOUT RAIN? I MEAN, WITHOUT RAINWATER?
WHY, THEY DRINK EMO-BUBBLES, OF COURSE!
EMO-WHAT? ARE YOU JUST MAKING THIS UP?
NO! WHEN THE FABULIST TELLS HER STORY, THE FABULEMES CAUSE THE LISTENERS TO PRODUCE EMO-BUBBLES! THEN THE EMO-BUBBLES NOURISH THE TEAR-EATERS!
WE'VE NEVER HEARD THOSE WORDS BEFORE!
HUH?
THE FABULEMES HELP THE FABULIST TELL STORIES. THESE STORIES ARE SO BEAUTIFUL THAT PEOPLE CAN'T HELP BUT SHED EMO-BUBBLES.
THE RAIN WILL BE STOPPING SOON. LET'S GO HEAR THIS EVENING'S STORY. THEN YOU'LL UNDERSTAND!

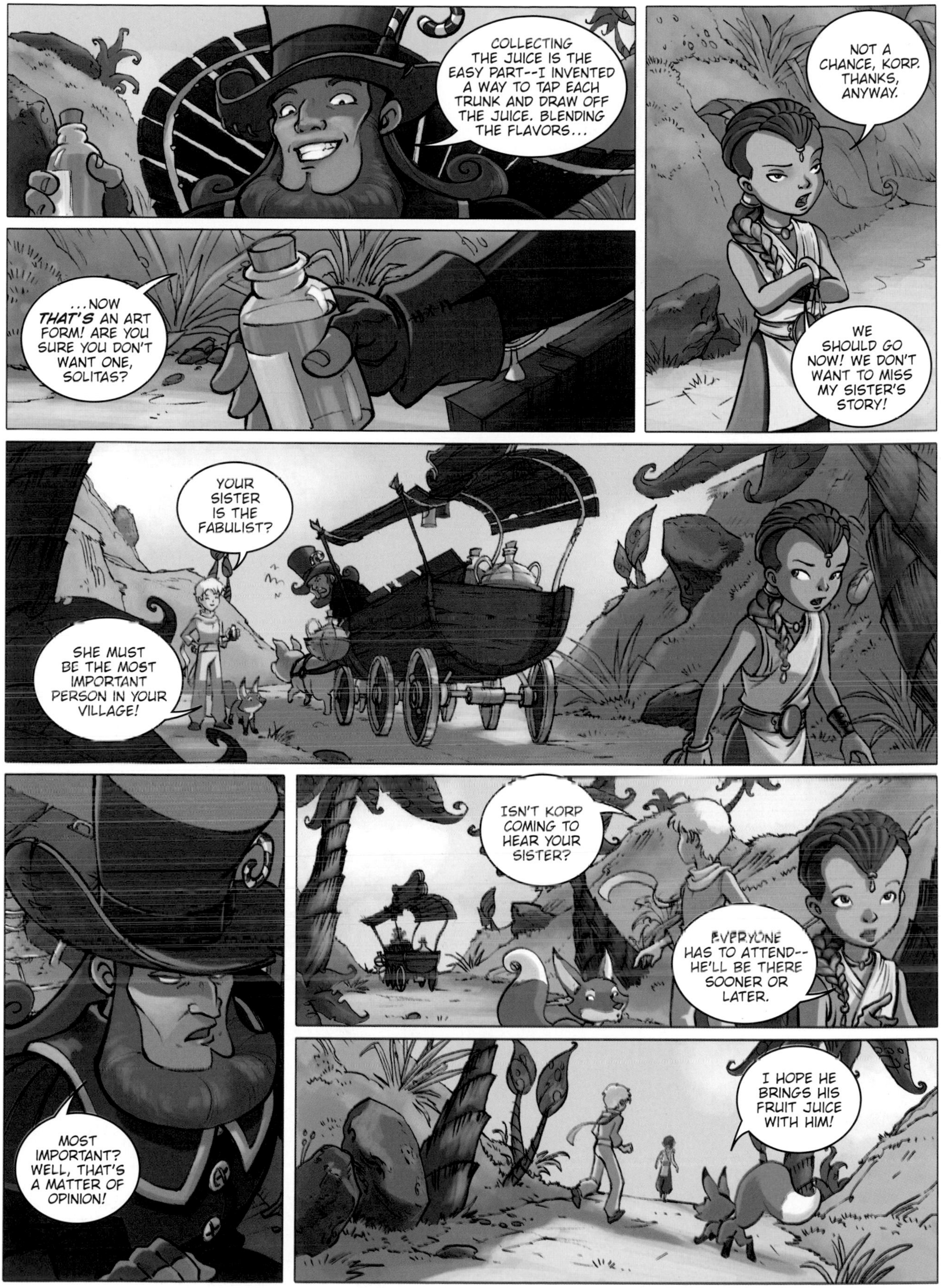
COLLECTING THE JUICE IS THE EASY PART--I INVENTED A WAY TO TAP EACH TRUNK AND DRAW OFF THE JUICE. BLENDING THE FLAVORS...
...NOW THAT'S AN ART FORM! ARE YOU SURE YOU DON'T WANT ONE, SOLITAS?
NOT A CHANCE, KORP. THANKS, ANYWAY.
WE SHOULD GO NOW! WE DON'T WANT TO MISS MY SISTER'S STORY!
YOUR SISTER IS THE FABULIST?
SHE MUST BE THE MOST IMPORTANT PERSON IN YOUR VILLAGE!
MOST IMPORTANT? WELL, THAT'S A MATTER OF OPINION!
ISN'T KORP COMING TO HEAR YOUR SISTER?
EVERYONE HAS TO ATTEND--HE'LL BE THERE SOONER OR LATER.
I HOPE HE BRINGS HIS FRUIT JUICE WITH HIM!

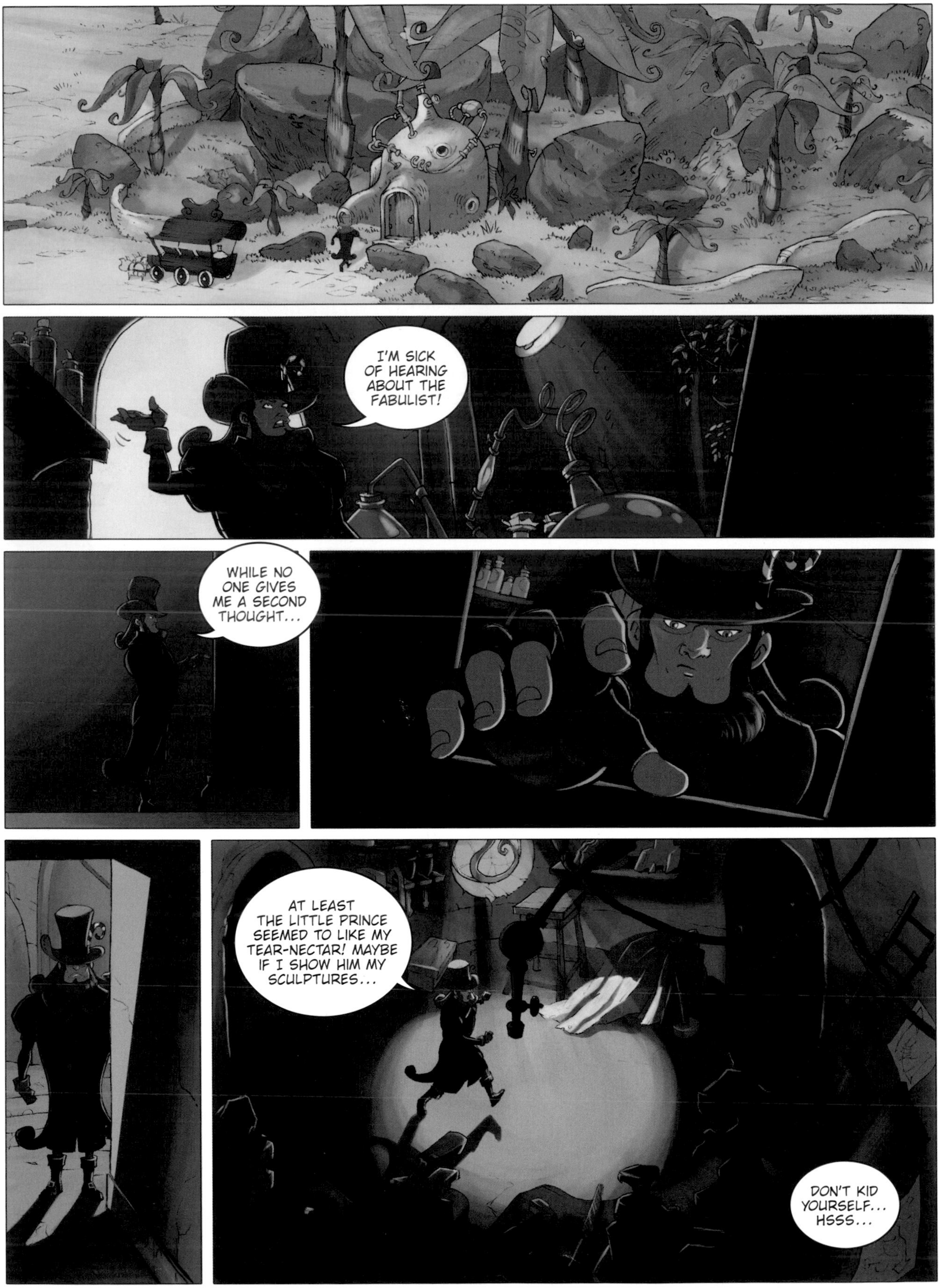
I'M SICK OF HEARING ABOUT THE FABULIST!
WHILE NO ONE GIVES ME A SECOND THOUGHT...
AT LEAST THE LITTLE PRINCE SEEMED TO LIKE MY TEAR-NECTAR! MAYBE IF I SHOW HIM MY SCULPTURES...
DON'T KID YOURSELF... HSSS...

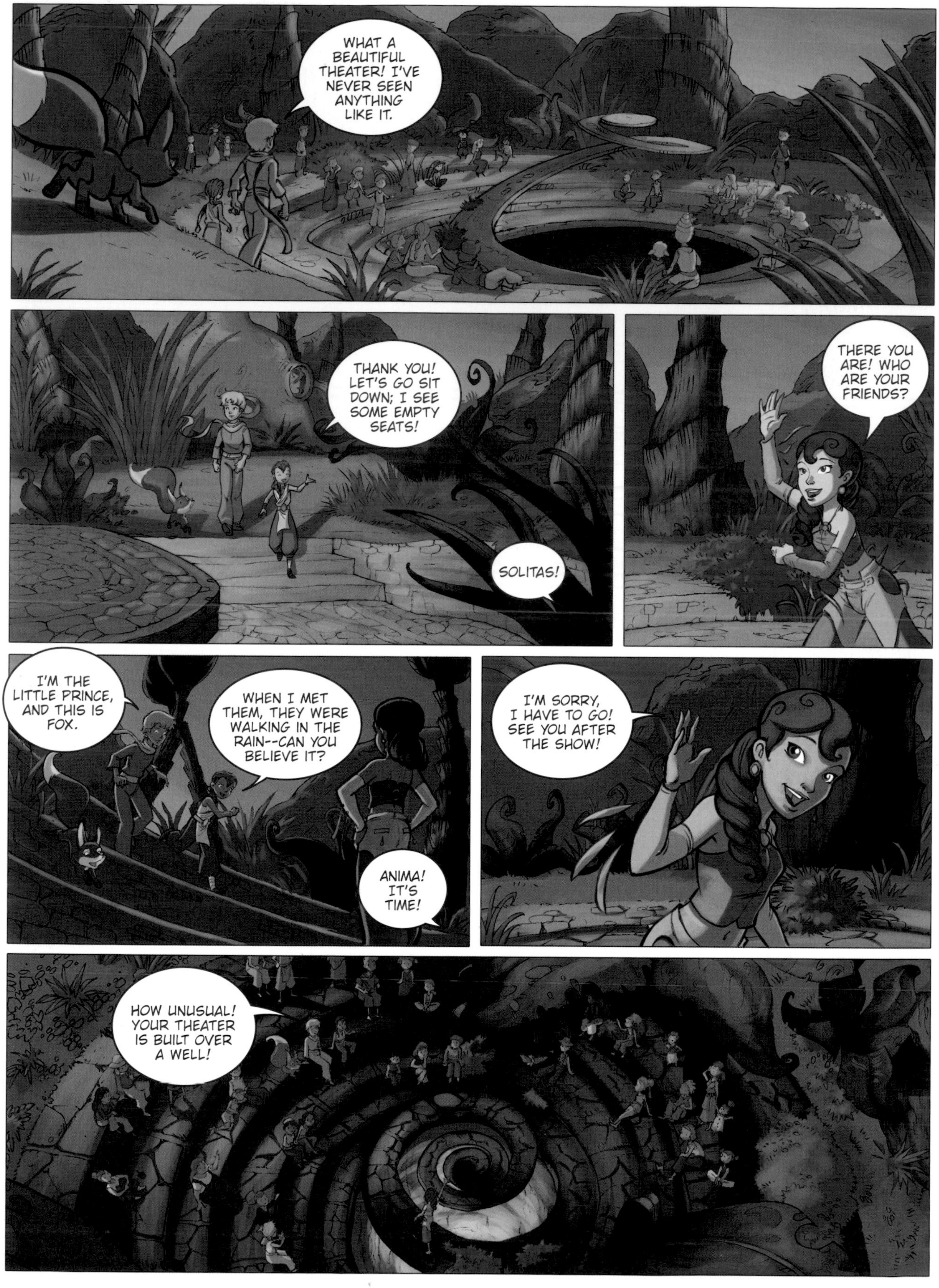
WHAT A BEAUTIFUL THEATER! I'VE NEVER SEEN ANYTHING LIKE IT.
THANK YOU! LET'S GO SIT DOWN; I SEE SOME EMPTY SEATS!
SOLITAS!
THERE YOU ARE! WHO ARE YOUR FRIENDS?
I'M THE LITTLE PRINCE, AND THIS IS FOX.
WHEN I MET THEM, THEY WERE WALKING IN THE RAIN--CAN YOU BELIEVE IT?
ANIMA! IT'S TIME!
I'M SORRY, I HAVE TO GO! SEE YOU AFTER THE SHOW!
HOW UNUSUAL! YOUR THEATER IS BUILT OVER A WELL!

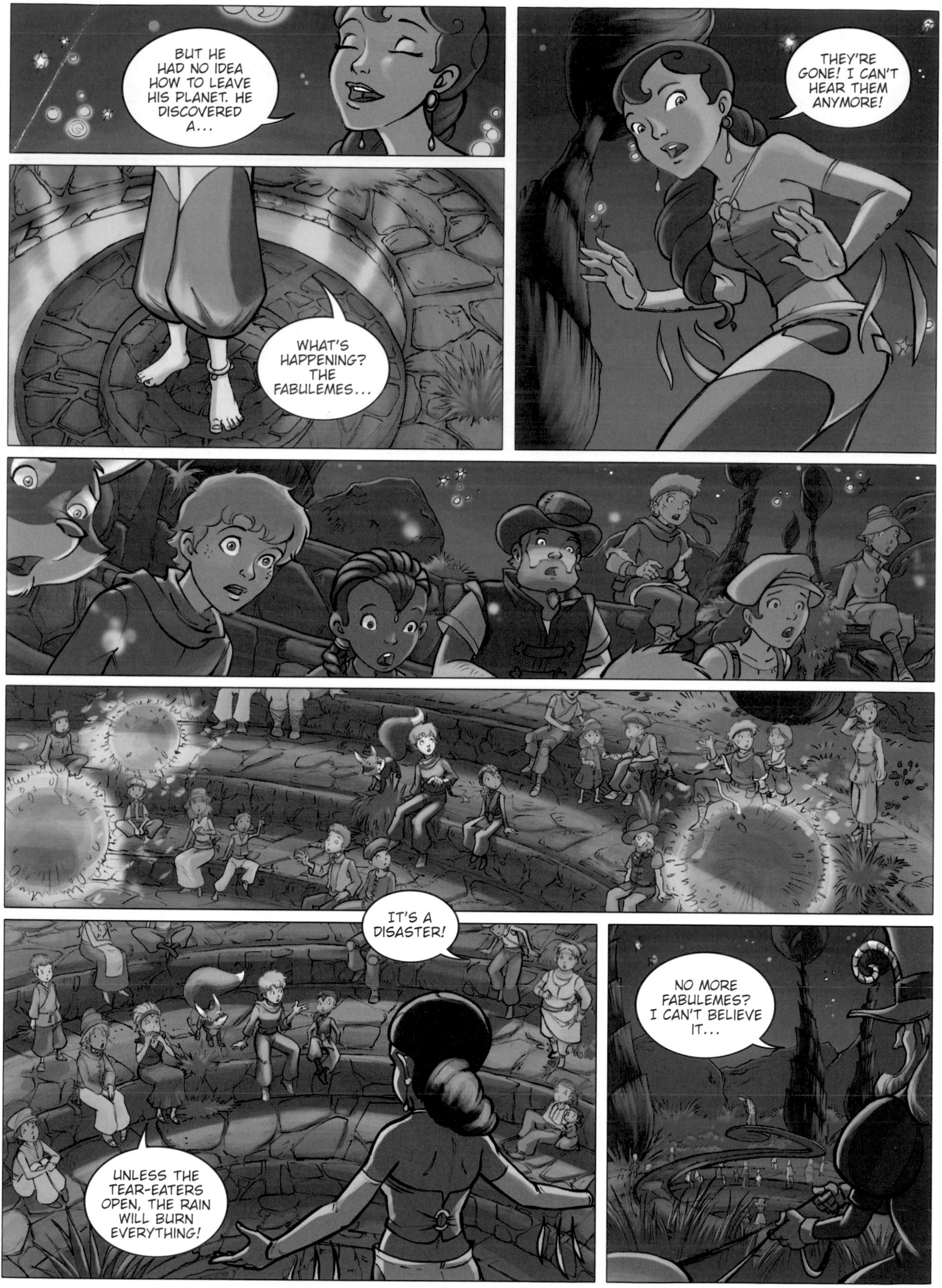
BUT HE HAD NO IDEA HOW TO LEAVE HIS PLANET. HE DISCOVERED A...
WHAT'S HAPPENING? THE FABULEMES...
THEY'RE GONE! I CAN'T HEAR THEM ANYMORE!
IT'S A DISASTER!
UNLESS THE TEAR-EATERS OPEN, THE RAIN WILL BURN EVERYTHING!
NO MORE FABULEMES? I CAN'T BELIEVE IT...

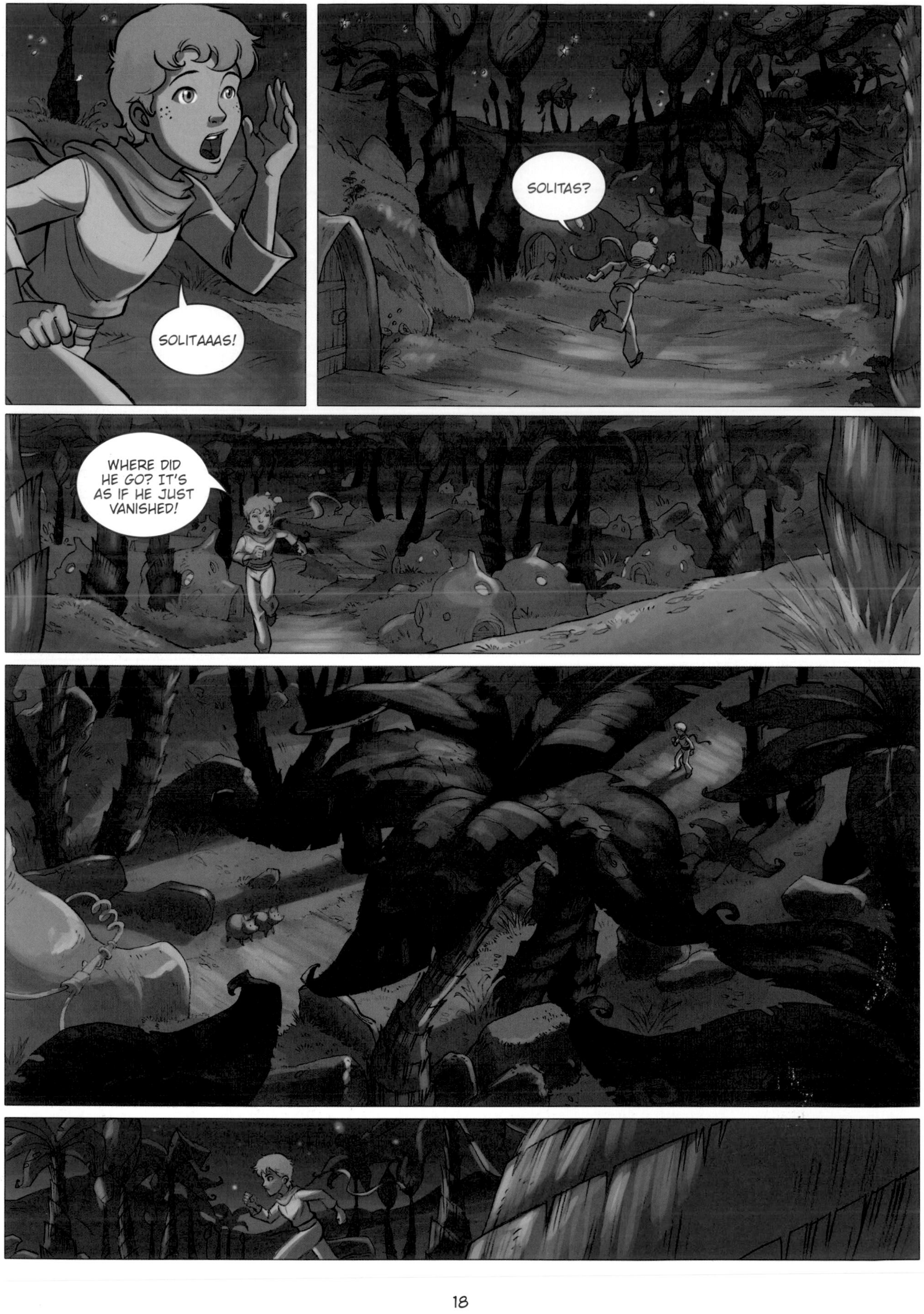
SOLITAAAS!
SOLITAS?
WHERE DID HE GO? IT'S AS IF HE JUST VANISHED!

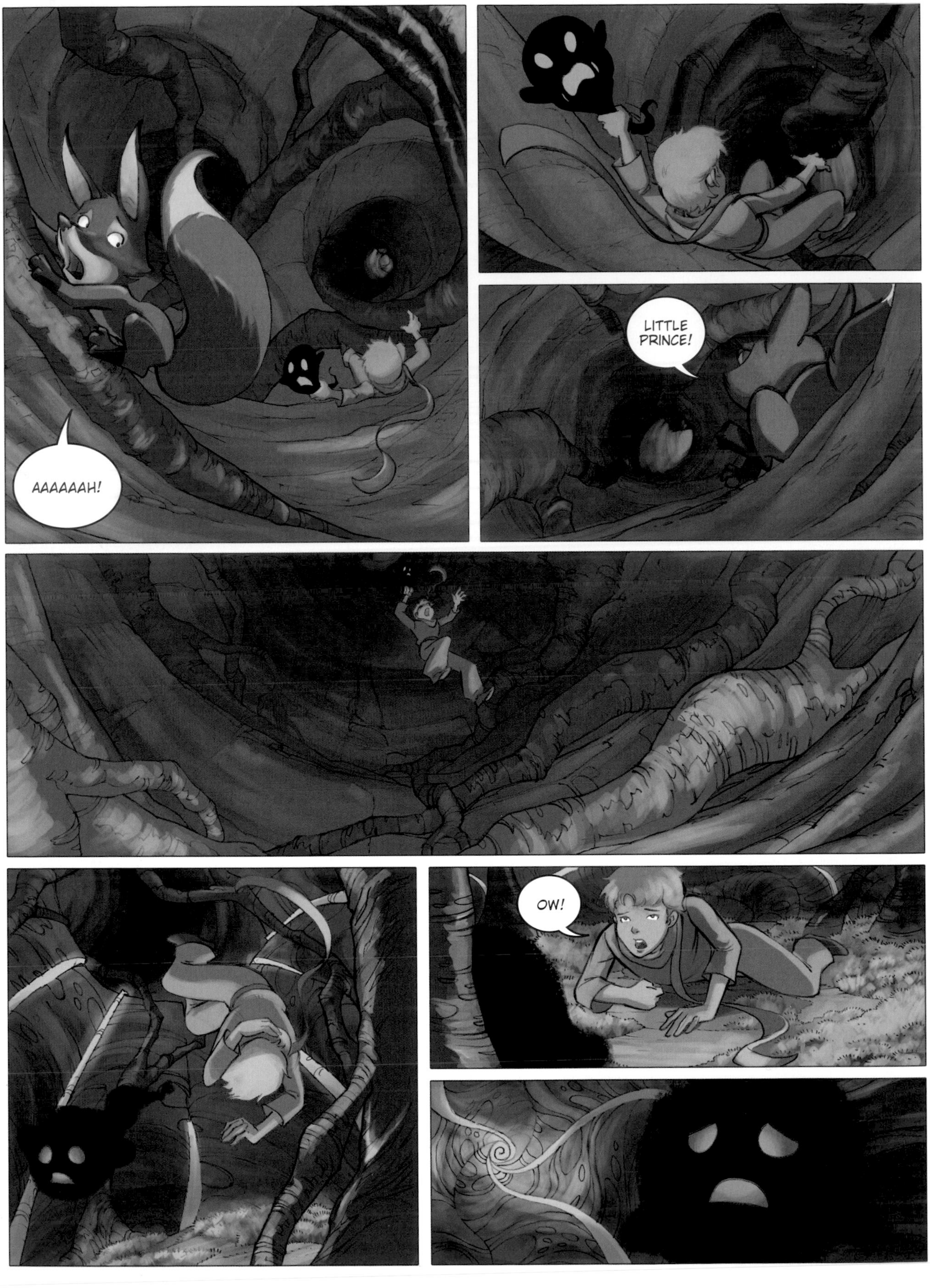
AAAAAAH!
LITTLE PRINCE!
OW!

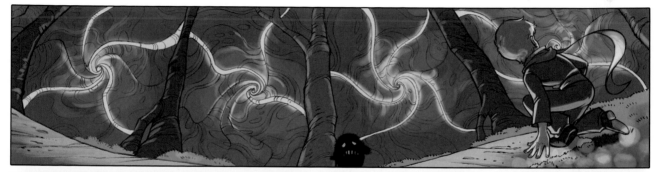

FOX?

IT'S A MAZE!

YOU!

I HAVE AN IDEA...

THE DOORS ONLY OPEN WHEN I APPROACH THEM. WITHOUT ME, YOU'RE TRAPPED!

NOW, I FIGURED OUT HOW YOU ALWAYS APPEAR WITHOUT WARNING...

YOU CAN FIND US ANYWHERE, CAN'T YOU?

HELP ME FIND FOX, AND I'LL HELP YOU GET OUT!

SO, DO WE HAVE A DEAL?

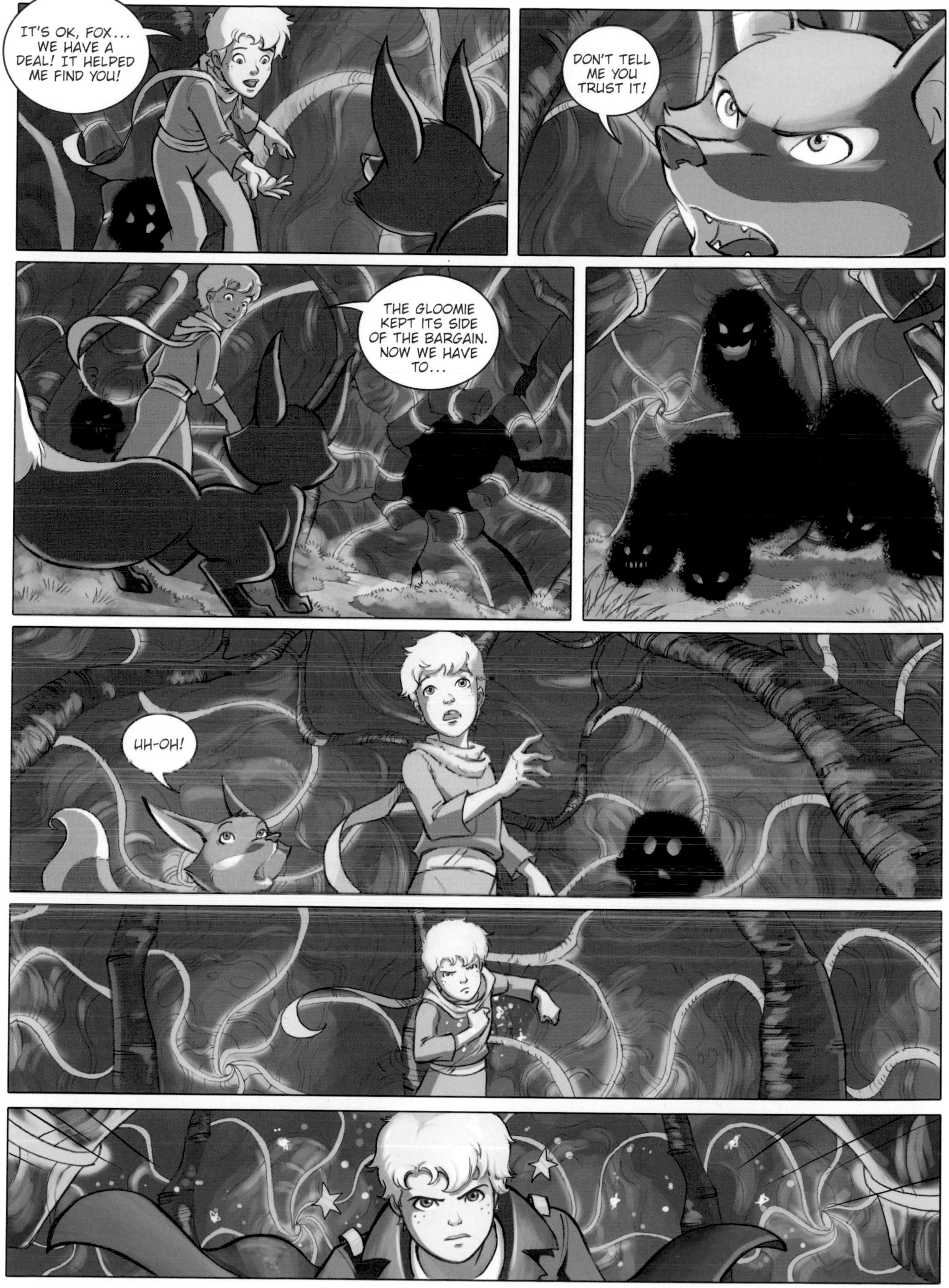
IT'S OK, FOX... WE HAVE A DEAL! IT HELPED ME FIND YOU!
DON'T TELL ME YOU TRUST IT!
THE GLOOMIE KEPT ITS SIDE OF THE BARGAIN. NOW WE HAVE TO...
UH-OH!

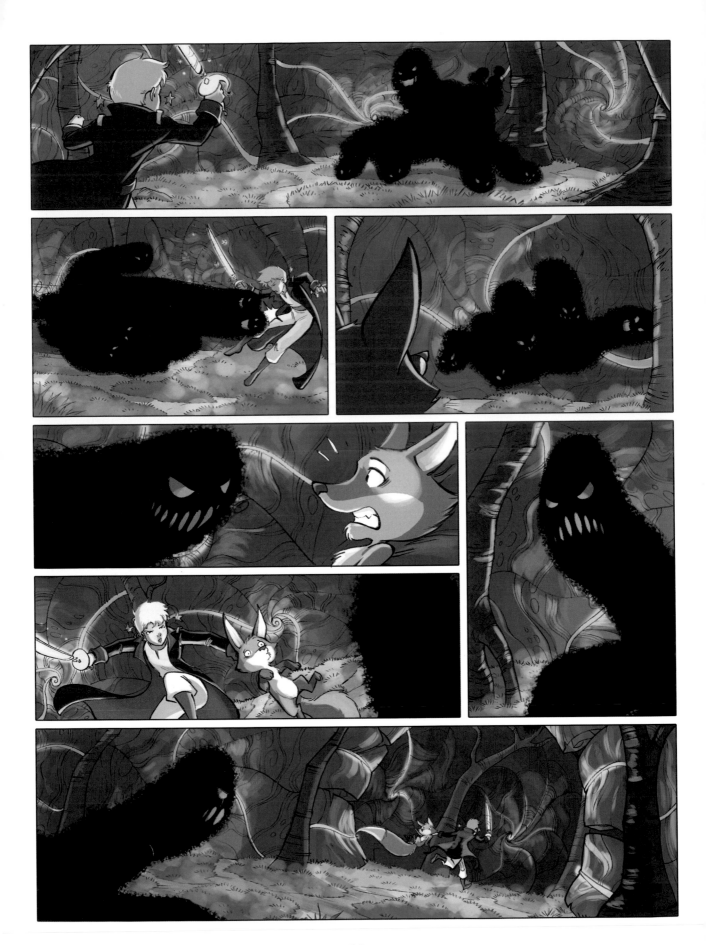

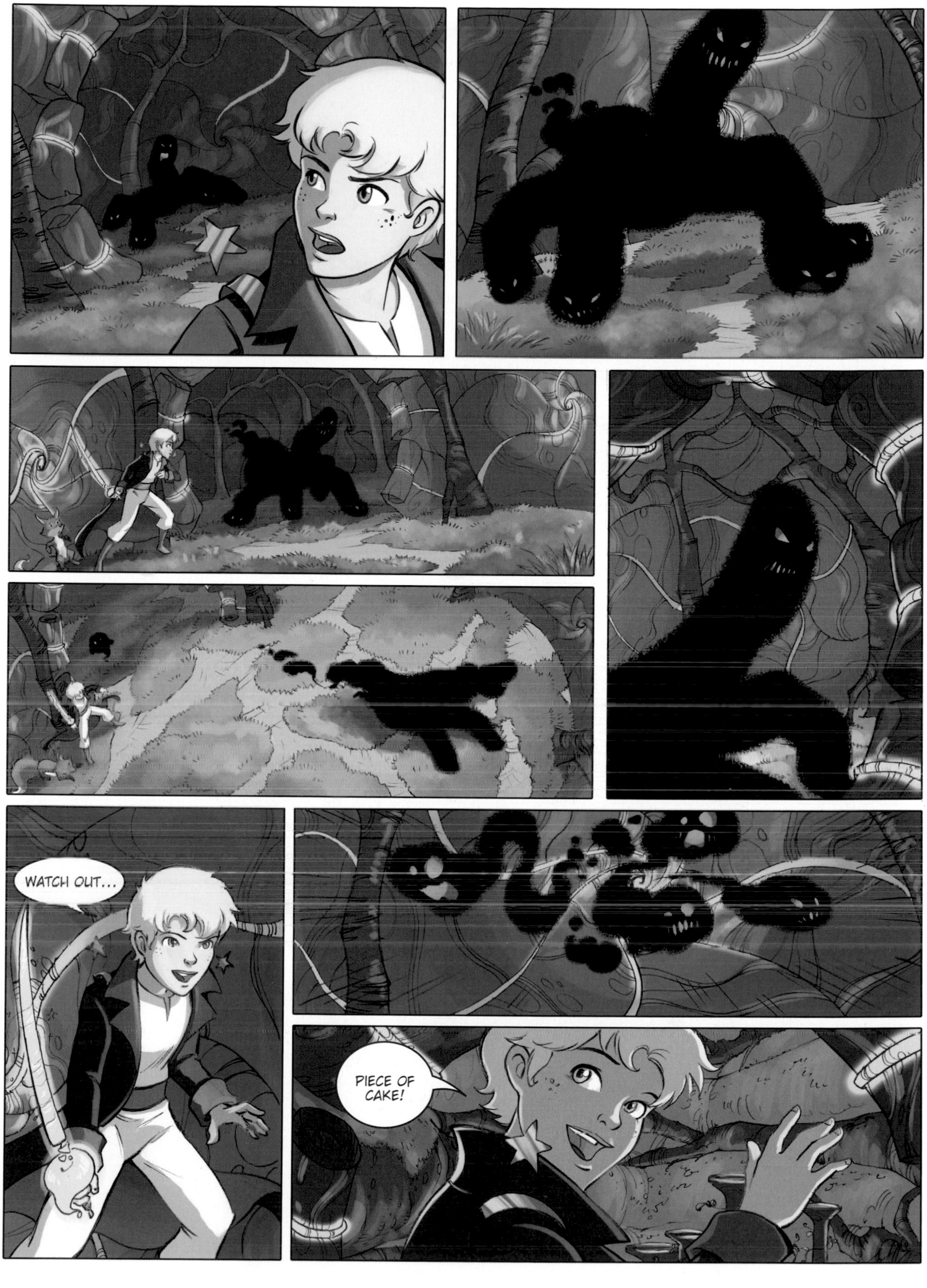
WATCH OUT...
PIECE OF CAKE!

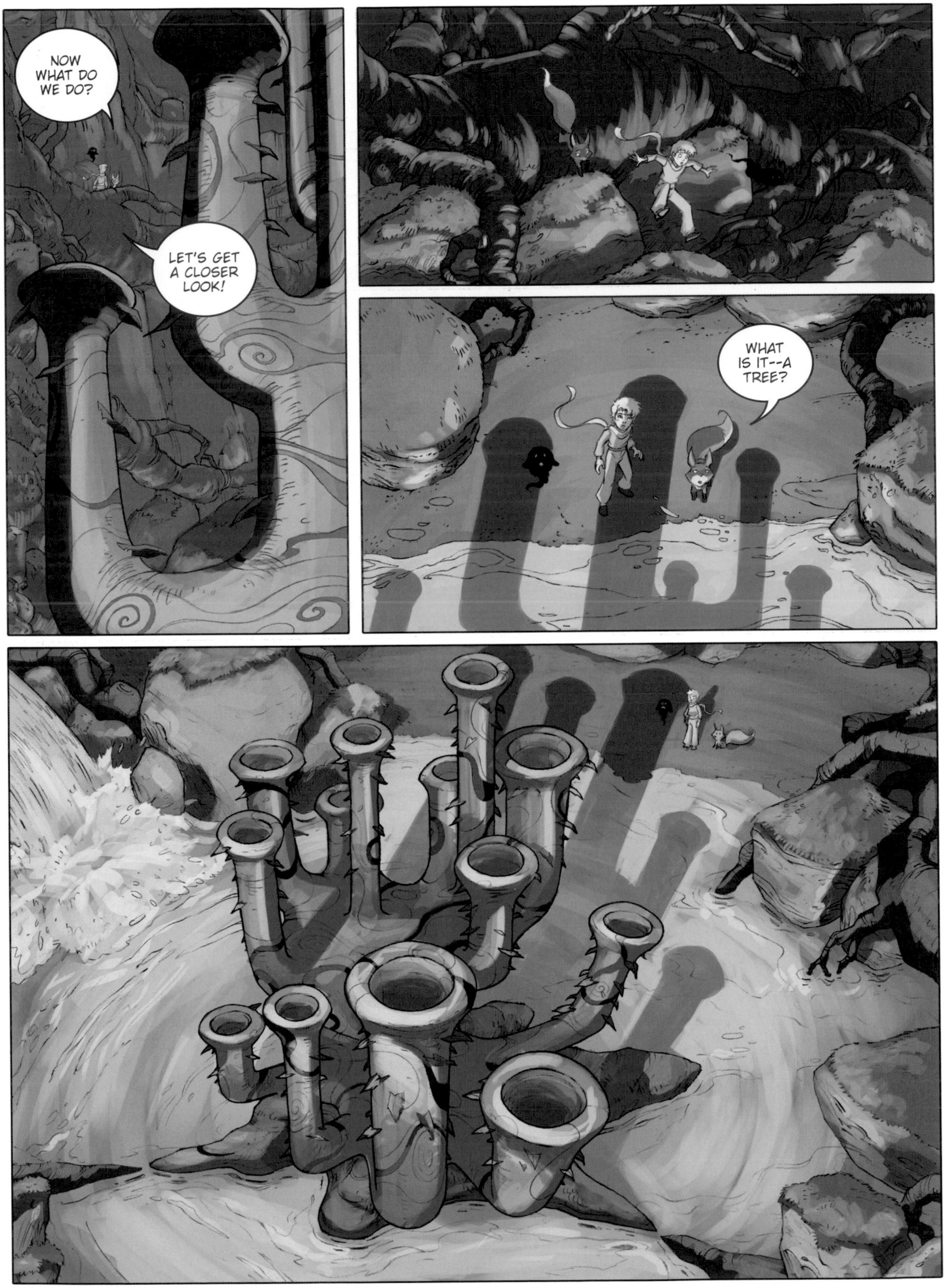
NOW WHAT DO WE DO?
LET'S GET A CLOSER LOOK!
WHAT IS IT--A TREE?

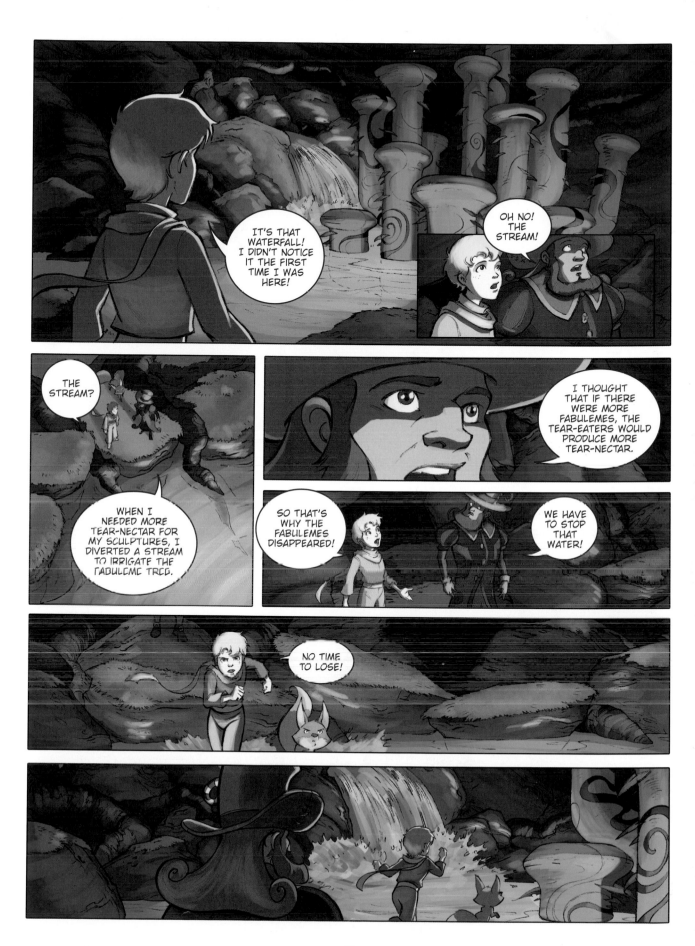

41

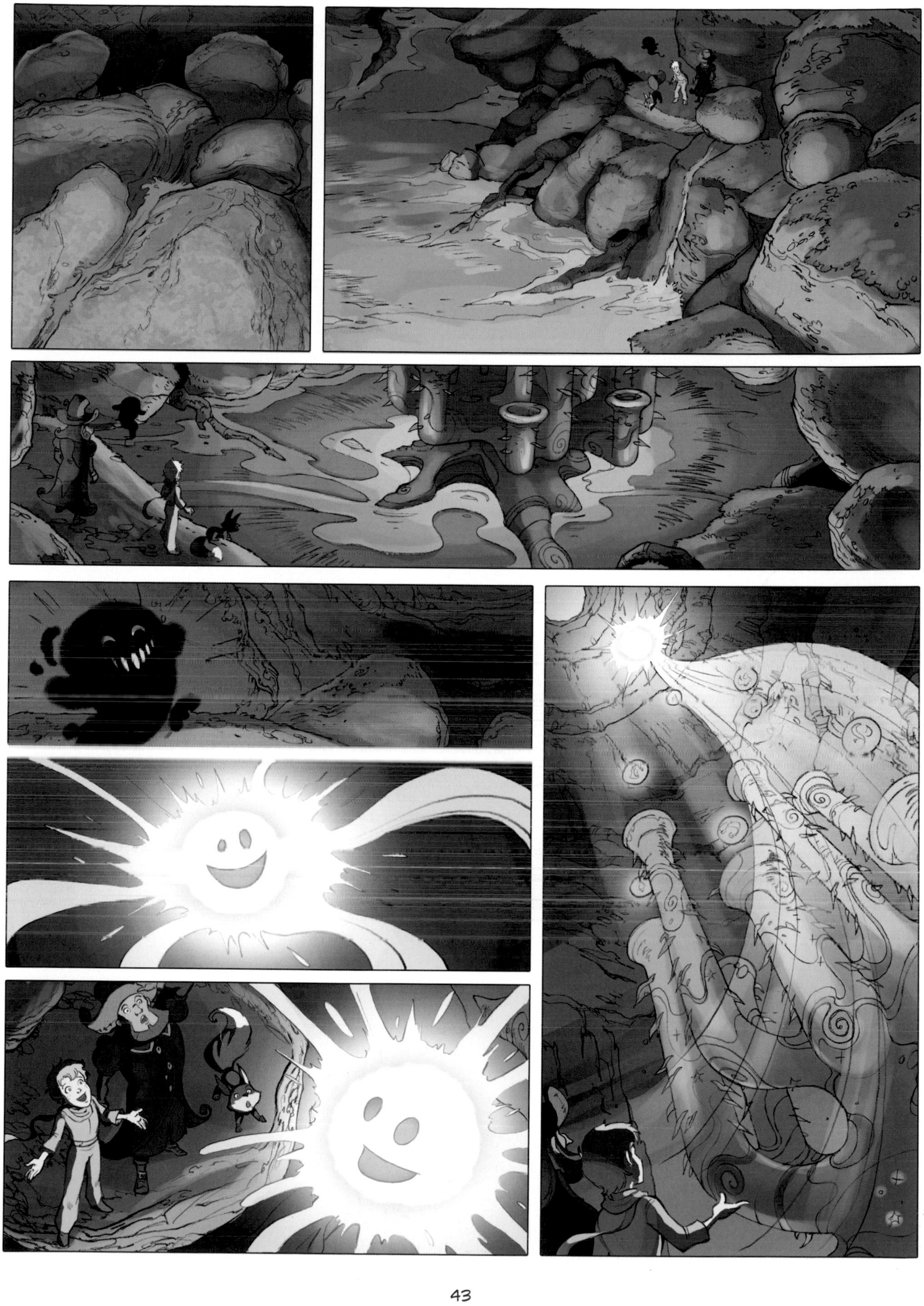

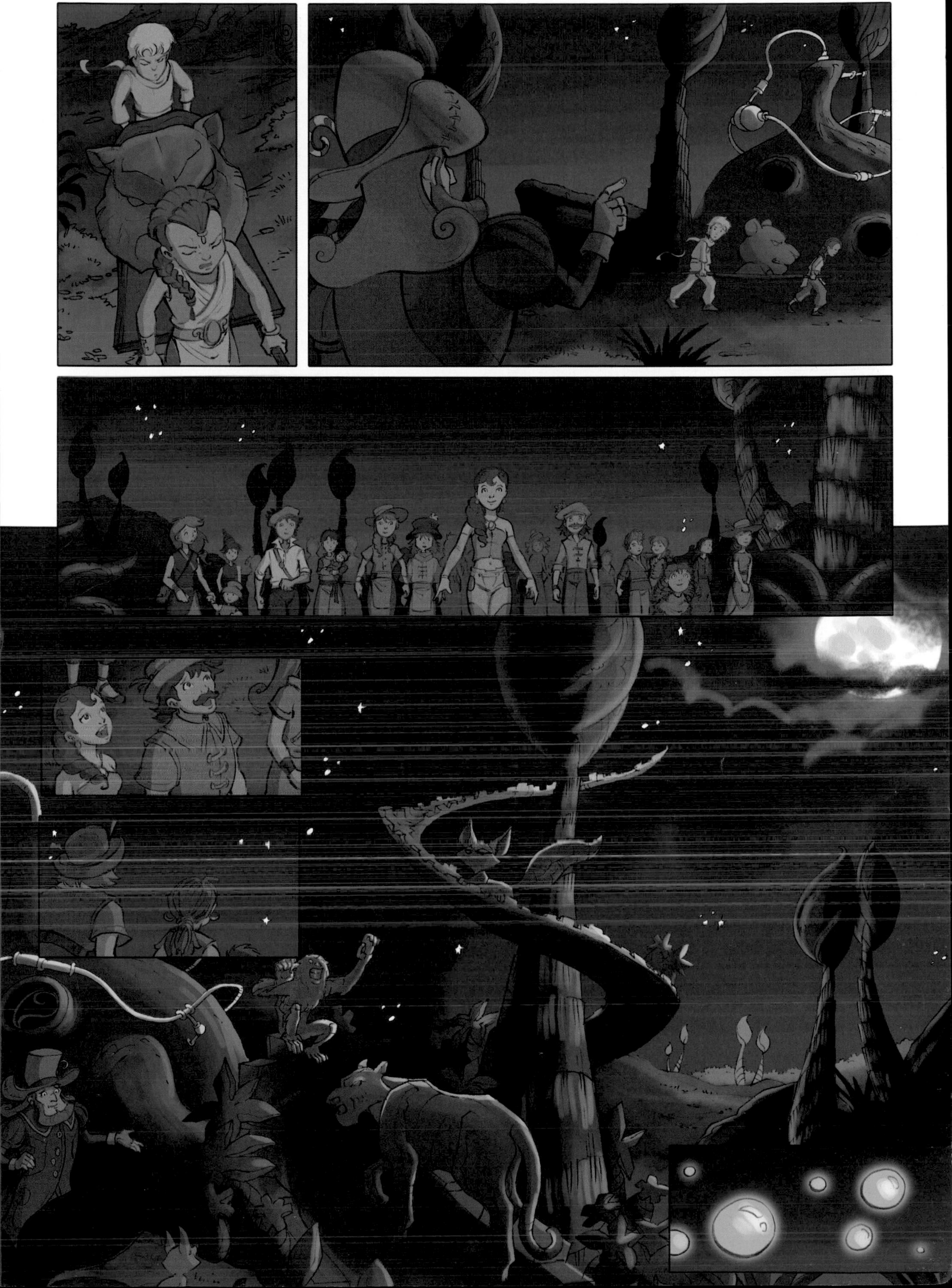

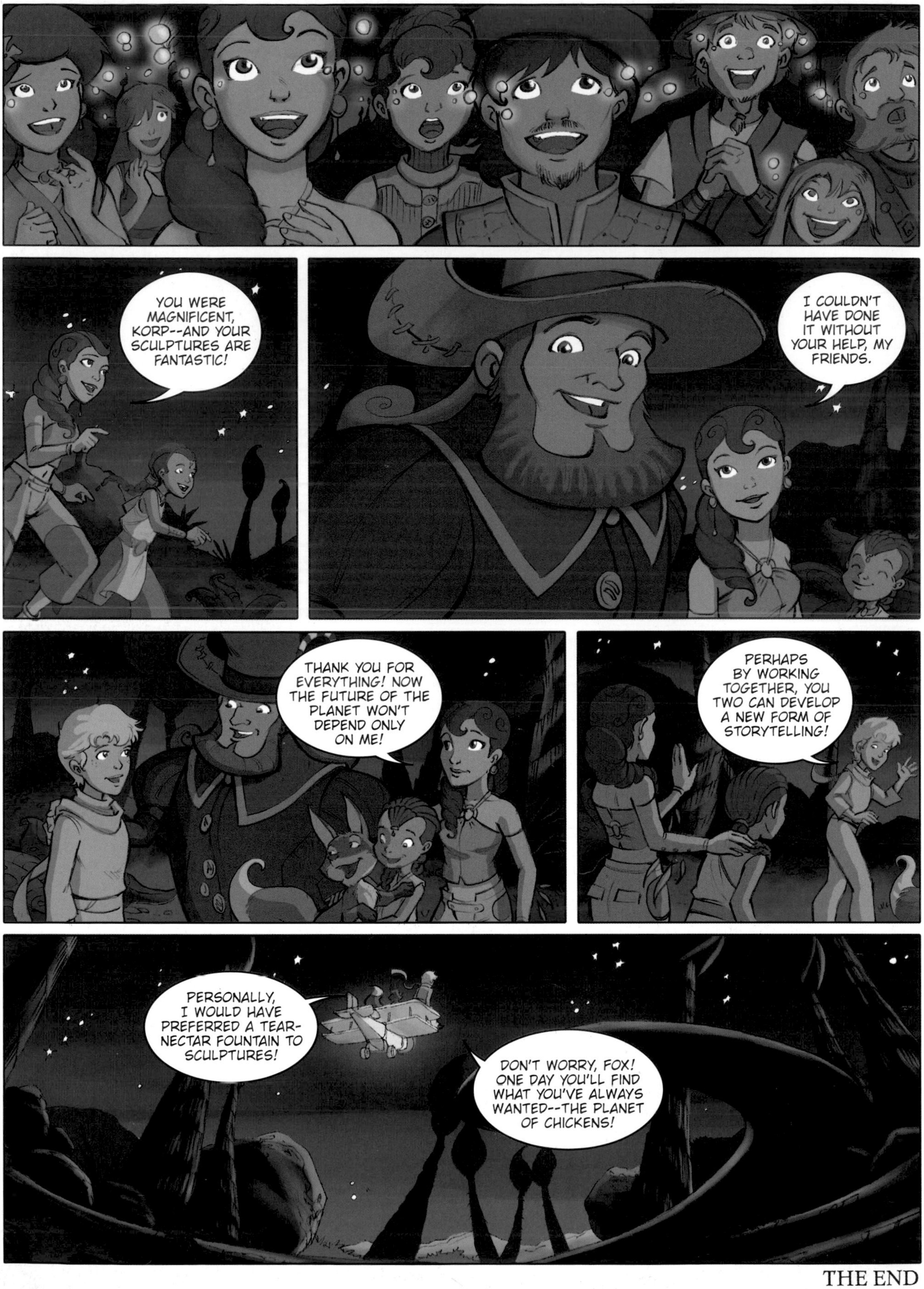
YOU WERE MAGNIFICENT, KORP--AND YOUR SCULPTURES ARE FANTASTIC!
I COULDN'T HAVE DONE IT WITHOUT YOUR HELP, MY FRIENDS.
THANK YOU FOR EVERYTHING! NOW THE FUTURE OF THE PLANET WON'T DEPEND ONLY ON ME!
PERHAPS BY WORKING TOGETHER, YOU TWO CAN DEVELOP A NEW FORM OF STORYTELLING!
PERSONALLY, I WOULD HAVE PREFERRED A TEAR-NECTAR FOUNTAIN TO SCULPTURES!
DON'T WORRY, FOX! ONE DAY YOU'LL FIND WHAT YOU'VE ALWAYS WANTED--THE PLANET OF CHICKENS!

THE END

BOOK 1: THE PLANET OF WIND

BOOK 2: THE PLANET OF THE FIREBIRD

BOOK 3: THE PLANET OF MUSIC

BOOK 4: THE PLANET OF JADE

BOOK 5: THE STAR SNATCHER'S PLANET

BOOK 6: THE PLANET OF THE NIGHT GLOBES

BOOK 7: THE PLANET OF THE OVERHEARERS

BOOK 8: THE PLANET OF THE TORTOISE DRIVER

BOOK 9: THE PLANET OF THE GIANT

BOOK 10: THE PLANET OF TRAINIACS

BOOK 11: THE PLANET OF LIBRIS

BOOK 12: THE PLANET OF LUDOKAA

BOOK 13: THE PLANET OF TEAR-EATERS

BOOK 14: THE PLANET OF THE GRAND BUFFOON

BOOK 15: THE PLANET OF THE GARGAND

BOOK 16: THE PLANET OF GEHOM

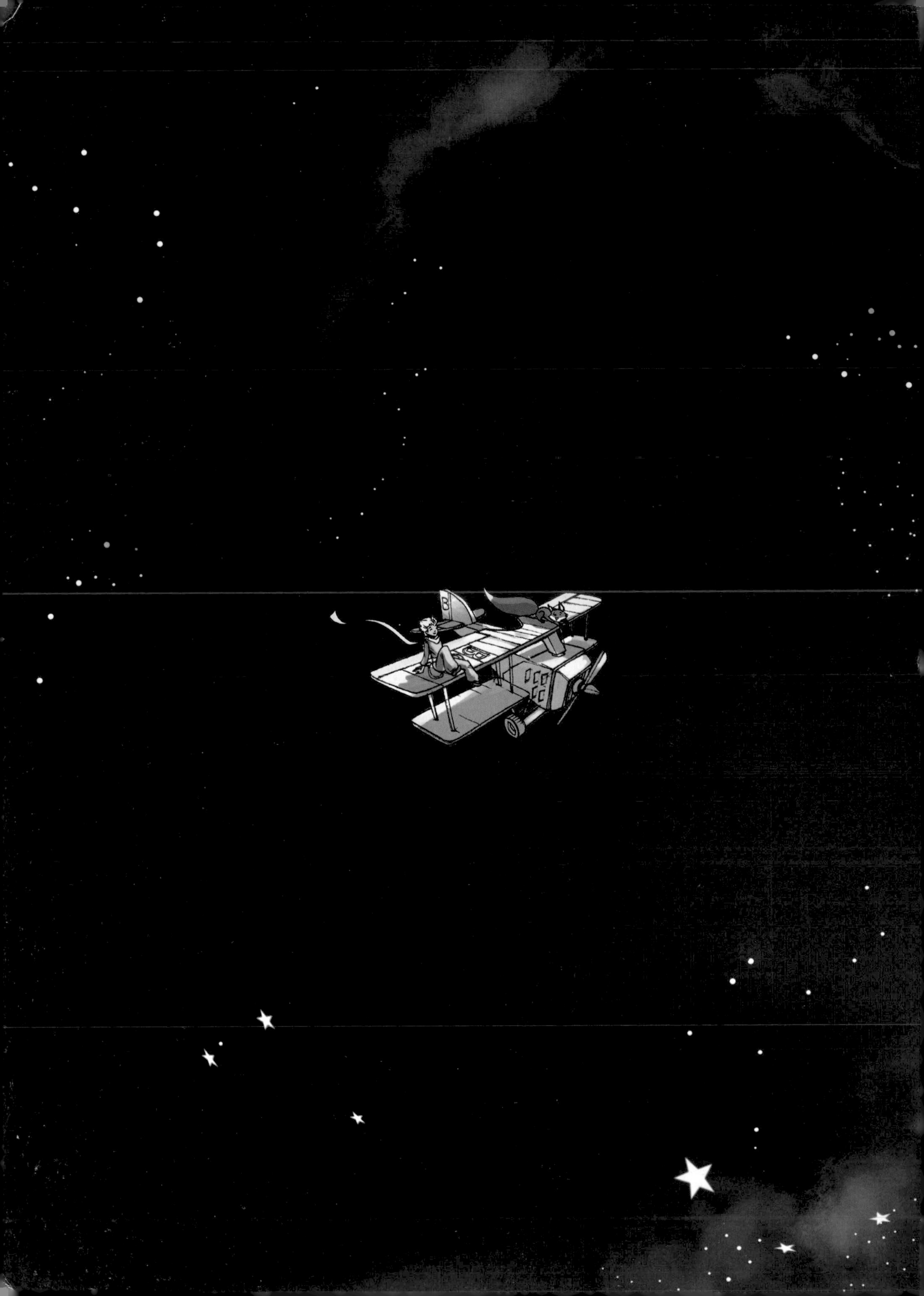